NANCY DREW
AND THE CLUE CREW

#36

The Secret
of the
Scarecrow

The last
straw!

CAROLYN KEENE   ILLUSTRATED BY MACKY PAMINTUAN

Crack these other cases!

A Big Scare!

Nancy, Bess, and George found a still-barking Chip in the living room, her paws against the windowsill.

"She's barking at something outside," Bess said.

"It's probably a deer," Nancy said.

The girls peered out the window. It was getting dark early.

"That doesn't look like an animal to me," George said.

Nancy looked closer until she saw what George meant. A small, shadowy figure was dancing across her front yard wearing baggy clothes and a big hat!

"Who was that?" Nancy said as he ran away.

"You mean *what*?" George said slowly. "Baggy clothes, huge hat—I think we just saw a scarecrow."

"Yeah." Bess gulped. "A real *live* scarecrow!"

Join the CLUE CREW
& solve these other cases!

NANCY DREW
AND THE CLUE CREW®

#36

The Secret of the
Scarecrow

BY CAROLYN KEENE

ILLUSTRATED BY MACKY PAMINTUAN

Aladdin

New York   London   Toronto   Sydney   New Delhi

🫖 ALADDIN
An imprint of Simon & Schuster Children's Publishing Division
1230 Avenue of the Americas, New York, NY 10020
First Aladdin paperback edition November 2013
Text copyright © 2013 by Simon and Schuster, Inc.
Illustrations copyright © 2013 by Macky Pamintuan
All rights reserved, including the right of reproduction in whole or in part in any form.
ALADDIN and related logo, NANCY DREW, and NANCY DREW AND THE CLUE CREW are registered trademarks of Simon & Schuster, Inc.
For information about special discounts for bulk purchases, please contact Simon & Schuster Special Sales at 1-866-506-1949 or business@simonandschuster.com.
The Simon & Schuster Speakers Bureau can bring authors to your live event.
For more information or to book an event contact the Simon & Schuster Speakers Bureau at 1-866-248-3049 or visit our website at www.simonspeakers.com.
Designed by Lisa Vega
The text of this book was set in ITC Stone Informal.
Manufactured in the United States of America 1013 OFF
10 9 8 7 6 5 4 3 2 1
Library of Congress Control Number 2012949908
ISBN 978-1-4424-5353-1
ISBN 978-1-4424-5355-5 (eBook)

CONTENTS

CHAPTER ONE

Surprise in Store

"Guess what, class?" Mrs. Ramirez said. "We have a special guest today."

Eight-year-old Nancy Drew smiled as she sat up straight behind her desk. She loved special guests almost as much as she loved solving mysteries. But who was the well-dressed woman standing next to Mrs. Ramirez?

Nancy's best friend Bess Marvin tugged gently at Nancy's reddish blond ponytail. "Who do you think she is, Nancy?" she whispered.

"I may be a detective," Nancy whispered back. "But I don't have a clue."

Nancy was lucky to have both of her best friends in her class. Her other best friend, George

Fayne, sat a few desks down. She was too far to trade whispers but close enough to trade smiles!

"My name is Mimi Franklin," the mystery guest said. "And I'm the owner of Darcy's Department Store."

"Wow," Nancy said under her breath. Darcy's was the biggest store in River Heights!

"Has anyone here shopped at Darcy's?" Ms. Franklin asked.

Nancy's hand shot up. Her new back-to-school shoes were bought at Darcy's. She looked around the classroom to see all hands up. All except Leanne Hudson's.

"You've never shopped at Darcy's?" Ms. Franklin asked Leanne.

"No," Leanne Hudson said. She added quickly, "But Hudson's Apparel is having a sale on suitcases and duffel bags!"

Nancy got it. Leanne's parents owned Hudson's Apparel, a smaller store across the street from Darcy's. Why would she shop anywhere else?

"Ms. Franklin is here to tell us about her special surprise," Mrs. Ramirez said. "Go ahead, Ms. Franklin."

Nancy sat up even straighter. What could it be?

"Darcy's is about to decorate their store windows for fall," Ms. Franklin explained. "There'll be pumpkins, colorful fall leaves, and a scarecrow."

Ms. Franklin gave a big smile and said, "Mrs. Ramirez is a friend of mine, and she tells me how creative this class is . . . so how would you like to make our scarecrow?"

Excited whispers filled the room.

"What kind of scarecrow?" George asked.

"Any kind," Ms. Franklin said. "As long as it's no bigger than a nine-year-old and is wearing clothes from Darcy's."

Tommy Maron's hand shot up. "Does Darcy's sell superhero capes?" he asked.

"Uh . . . no," Ms. Franklin said.

"Phooey," Tommy grumbled.

Mrs. Ramirez explained the next step: "Each of you will draw an idea for the scarecrow. Then Ms. Franklin will pick the best one for their window."

Nancy smiled over her shoulder at Bess. A contest!

"Once I pick a winner, I will choose the outfit at Darcy's that best matches that design."

"You can work in teams," Mrs. Ramirez said. "But no more than three."

Perfect! Nancy thought. She, Bess, and George were already a team—a team of detectives who called themselves the Clue Crew.

"Is everybody ready to make a scarecrow?" Ms. Franklin asked.

"Not me," a voice in the back said.

Everyone turned to see Harvey Mueller.

"Scarecrows are scary for a reason," Harvey said. "Haven't you guys heard of Jake McStuffings?"

"Jake Mc-who?" Kevin Garcia asked.

"Jake's a scarecrow who wears baggy overalls and a big straw hat," Harvey said in a hushed voice. "Every fall, Jake leaps off his pole to wander the streets of River Heights."

Most of the kids snickered. Harvey was always making up scary stories!

"Quit laughing!" Harvey said. "Jake is for real!"

Mrs. Ramirez clapped her hands for attention.

"Okay, class," Mrs. Ramirez said. "Let's go quietly to the art room so we can begin."

The kids formed a line near the door. Nancy stood with Bess and George. She frowned when Deirdre Shannon stepped behind her. Deirdre was spoiled and usually got whatever she wanted. What she wanted now was to win the contest!

"I have the best idea for a scarecrow," Deirdre bragged loudly. "But I'm not telling."

As they filed out of the room George whispered, "I don't know who's scarier—Jake McStuffings or Deirdre!"

"I heard that, *Georgia* Fayne!" Deirdre snapped.

Nancy watched George's dark eyes flash. Nobody used her real name except her grandmother—and Deirdre Shannon!

The art room had its usual paint-and-clay smell as the class filed in. Nancy, Bess, and George ran to an easel set up with paper and colored pencils.

"What should our scarecrow look like?" Nancy asked.

"Totally fashion forward!" Bess said.

"How about a computerized scarecrow?" George suggested. "He can wear blinking lights and maybe talk!"

"It's a scarecrow, not a robot!" Bess argued.

George heaved a sigh. "Sometimes I can't believe we're cousins, Bess."

Neither could Nancy. Bess had blond hair and blue eyes and loved clothes more than anything. George had dark hair and eyes. She loved computers . . . and clothes, too—as long as they were comfortable enough to do cartwheels in.

"Here's my idea," Bess said. She quickly drew a scarecrow. Over it she drew a dark red coat, black leggings, yellow boots, and a hat decorated with flowers.

"Pretty!" Nancy swooned.

"Not bad," George admitted.

When everyone was done, Ms. Franklin checked out the drawings. Nadine Nardo, Kendra Jackson, and Marcy Rubin designed a sleepover scarecrow wearing colorful pj's. Peter Patino, Quincy Taylor, and Kevin Garcia were proud of their scarecrow wearing sports clothes and sneakers.

"After our scarecrow is in the window," Quincy explained, "he can be the mascot for our soccer team—the Green Monsters!"

Next Ms. Franklin checked out Harvey's sketch. His scarecrow looked just like Jake McStuffings, of course. Leanne's scarecrow was nothing but a stick figure.

Nancy couldn't wait for Ms. Franklin to check out their scarecrow. But she wasn't the only one. . . .

"Look at my Hollywood scarecrow, Ms. Franklin," Deirdre called. "Isn't she glam enough for the red carpet?"

"Very nice, dear," Ms. Franklin said with a quick glance. She then breezed past Deirdre to Nancy, Bess, and George's easel.

Ms. Franklin studied the scarecrow in the flowered hat and yellow boots before flashing a huge smile. "That outfit is fabulous!" she cried. "And we have clothes just like that at Darcy's."

She then turned to the class and said, "You all did an amazing job, kids, but I believe we have a winner."

"Yippee!" Nancy cheered.

"Not fair!" Deirdre snapped while Nancy, Bess, and George high-fived. "They're detectives—not designers!"

"Now we're designing detectives." Bess smiled.

After the class quieted down, Mrs. Ramirez explained that they would build the scarecrow on Friday before the dismissal bell. That was only three days away!

"Darcy's will have the most stylish scarecrow ever!" Ms. Franklin declared. "Thanks to Nancy, Bess, and George."

"Yeah," Deirdre muttered. "Thanks a lot."

Nancy, Bess, and George didn't have time for sore losers like Deirdre. They had just won a major contest—and that called for a milk-and-cookie celebration!

"Ready? Go!" Hannah called out.

Nancy, Bess, and George picked up their glasses of milk and began to drink. Until Hannah said—"Stop!"

The girls giggled as they quickly put down their glasses. They loved playing Hannah's stop-and-go game when they drank milk with their cookies.

Hannah Gruen was more than just the Drews' housekeeper. She had been just like a mother to Nancy ever since Nancy's own mom died, when Nancy was three. Hannah gave the best hugs and baked the most awesome oatmeal-raisin cookies!

"I like our scarecrow," George said between

chews. "But whatever happened to regular overalls and straw hats?"

"Overalls and straw hats?" Bess said, rolling her eyes. "George, that's so *Wizard of Oz*."

Nancy was about to take another sip when her puppy barked loudly in another room.

"What's up with Chocolate Chip?" Bess asked.

"Maybe she doesn't like being named after a cookie," George joked.

Nancy, Bess, and George found a still-barking Chip in the living room, her paws against the windowsill.

"She's barking at something outside," Bess said.

"It's probably a deer," Nancy said. "There are lots of deer around here in the fall."

The girls peered out the window. It was getting dark early.

"That doesn't look like an animal to me," George said.

Nancy looked closer until she saw what

George meant. A small, shadowy figure was dancing across her front yard wearing baggy clothes and a big hat!

"Who was that?" Nancy said as he ran away.

"You mean *what*?" George said slowly. "Baggy clothes, huge hat—I think we just saw a scare-crow."

"Yeah." Bess gulped. "A real *live* scarecrow!"

CHAPTER TWO

Jake or Fake?

"So? Did you see Jake McStuffings yet?" Harvey Mueller asked Nancy, Bess, and George.

It was Friday afternoon. The kids of Mrs. Ramirez's class were in the school yard, ready to build a scarecrow.

"No, Harvey," Nancy insisted. "We didn't see Jake."

Harvey shrugged and walked away.

"But we did see a walking scarecrow, Nancy," Bess said. "Just a few days ago in your yard, remember?"

"I remember," Nancy admitted. "But it was getting dark, so we might have just seen a shadow."

"The shadow of a walking scarecrow," George muttered.

The kids had everything they needed for their scarecrow: arts-and-crafts supplies, a bale of hay, and the clothes from Darcy's Department Store.

Everyone was there except for Leanne. She had told Mrs. Ramirez she was allergic to hay, so she was excused to the library.

When it was finally time to build the scarecrow, everyone had a special job. Nancy, Bess, and George carefully pulled the clothes out of the bag. They looked very much like the clothes they had designed—except for the Darcy's label sewn inside each one.

"These clothes are awesome!" Bess exclaimed.

"You mean awful!" a voice sneered.

Nancy looked up to see Kevin, Peter, and Quincy. The boys were sticking their fingers in their mouths and making gagging noises.

"What's your problem?" George demanded.

"Whoever heard of a scarecrow with yellow

boots?" Kevin scoffed. "Our scarecrow should have been sporty."

"Yeah," Peter said. "Then he could have been our mascot too."

"Why don't you just get a new mascot for your soccer team?" Nancy asked.

"May I suggest a turkey?" George teased.

"Ha-ha," Quincy said, not laughing.

The girls were about to carry the clothes to Mrs. Ramirez when Deirdre called out, "Oh, goody! Here comes my special guest."

"Guest?" Mrs. Ramirez asked.

Everyone turned to see a young woman with bright red hair and sparkly-framed glasses walking over.

"Deirdre, who is she?" Mrs. Ramirez asked.

"Meet Suki Anderson!" Deirdre said. "Suki was a contestant on the TV show *Catwalk Champ*. She came in second place."

"I'm also a friend of Deirdre's mom," Suki added.

Bess leaned over and whispered, "I watch *Catwalk Champ*. It's where people compete in a fashion design contest."

"I asked Suki to design some new clothes for our scarecrow," Deirdre went on. "Since the ones she has now are so lame."

Suki reached into a big bag she was holding. She smiled as she pulled out what looked like a dress made of dried fall leaves!

"Ta-daa!" Suki sang out. "What every well-dressed scarecrow will be wearing this year!"

Mrs. Ramirez and the students stared quietly at the leafy dress in Suki's hand. To Nancy it looked more like an arts-and-crafts project than a dress!

"And I thought the yellow boots were ugly," Kevin muttered.

"I made a hat, too," Suki said, digging into

her bag. "I hope you like acorns—"

"It's lovely, Ms. Anderson," Mrs. Ramirez said, cutting in. "But Mimi Franklin already sent us a very nice outfit, so that won't be necessary."

"Are you saying no to me?" Deirdre gasped.

"Sorry, Deirdre," Mrs. Ramirez said.

Deirdre's mouth became a thin line. Her face turned red. Nancy knew that look. It meant Deirdre was supermad!

"I hate Darcy's Department Store!" Deirdre declared. "I will never shop there again. Never, ever, ever!"

Suki hurriedly said good-bye and left the school yard. Deirdre stood to the side and pouted while the others built the scarecrow. Making a scarecrow was harder than Nancy or her friends had thought, but it was tons of fun!

Kendra, Marcy, and Nadine had the job of tying the leggings at the bottom with string. Then everyone took turns stuffing them with hay. When that was done, they stuck the legs into the yellow boots. After they filled the coat and attached the legs, it was time to make the scarecrow's head. That was done by packing a small burlap sack with hay and tying it closed at the bottom. A smiling face was drawn on the sack with colorful markers.

"And now—for the finishing touch!" Bess said, carefully placing the flowered hat on the scarecrow's head.

"Awesome!" Nancy swooned as she and her classmates applauded their work.

"Our scarecrow needs a name, too," Mrs. Ramirez said. "Can anyone think of a good one?"

"Scary Mary," Deirdre muttered.

"Hay-ley." Quincy laughed. "Get it? Get it?"

"Bride of Jake McStuffings," Harvey said slowly.

"I know," Shelby Metcalf said. "How about *Autumn*?"

Nancy, Bess, and George liked the name.

Everyone else liked Autumn too. Everyone except Deirdre, but she never liked anything she didn't think of.

"Ms. Franklin will pick Autumn up on Monday," Mrs. Ramirez said. "But where should we keep her over the weekend?"

"At my house, please!" Bess said. "My mom is picking me up after school and there's plenty of room in our car!"

"Well," Mrs. Ramirez said. "As long as you keep her inside the house at all times."

"I promise, I'll take good care of Autumn until Monday," Bess said, jumping up and down. "Supergood care!"

"Okay, Bess," Mrs. Ramirez agreed.

"Yippee!" Bess cheered.

"Double yippee!" Nancy cheered too.

Mrs. Ramirez helped the kids pack up the craft supplies and clean up the extra hay. They finished just in time for the dismissal bell.

Bess was about to lift Autumn off the ground

when Deirdre said, "Wait! I want to take a picture of Autumn!"

"Why do you want to take a picture?" Nancy asked.

"It's for my blog," Deirdre said. "I have told you about my very own blog, Dishing with Deirdre, haven't I?"

"About a gazillion times," George groaned.

Deirdre took out a tiny pink camera and snapped a picture of Autumn. Without saying good-bye she walked away.

"Whatever!" Bess said. She looked down at the scarecrow and smiled. "Come on, Autumn. We're going home!"

Mrs. Marvin's car was already parked outside the school. As the girls carried Autumn, George said, "Remember to take good care of her, Bess."

"I told you I would," Bess said. "Besides, who would want to hurt a scarecrow?"

Nancy could think of only one. Deirdre Shannon!

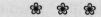

"Good morning, Sleeping Beauty!" Mr. Drew said.

Nancy smiled sleepily as she walked into the kitchen. Her dad was making his usual Saturday-morning pancakes. But this time they smelled a bit different.

"They're apple-cinnamon," Mr. Drew said, flipping one in the pan. "My latest fall recipe."

"Make sure it doesn't *fall* on the floor, Daddy!" Nancy giggled. Her dad was a great dad, a great lawyer, and a great cook—although a messy one!

Nancy was about to sit down when the phone on the kitchen counter rang. The caller ID flashed Bess's name.

"Hi, Bess," Nancy said as she answered the phone. "How's Autumn?"

"I don't know!" Bess cried.

"What do you mean, you don't know?" Nancy asked.

"All I know is that something happened to our scarecrow!" Bess said. "Something horrible!"

21

CHAPTER THREE

A Bess Mess

"What do you mean, something horrible?" Nancy asked worriedly. "Did someone steal her?"

"I don't know!" Bess cried. "I'll explain everything when you and George come over—right away!"

Nancy heard a click. Bess was so frantic, she had hung up without saying good-bye.

"Bad news?" Mr. Drew asked.

"I think so, Daddy," Nancy said. "Bess wants me to go to her house right away."

She was about to run for her jacket when she saw the yummy-looking stack of pancakes on the counter.

"Right away after pancakes!" Nancy added.

❀ ❀ ❀

"Okay, so where's Autumn?" George demanded.

"I don't know!" Bess wailed. "I left Autumn on the porch to run a quick errand with my mom this morning. When we came back, she was gone!"

"So you didn't keep her inside like you promised Mrs. Ramirez?" Nancy asked.

"I did! I did!" Bess said. "Except for the time she was out on the porch."

"Why was she out there?" Nancy asked.

"I wanted to see what a scarecrow would look like on our porch," Bess said. "I was going to put Autumn back inside, but then my mom called me from the car!"

"So you left her on the porch." George sighed. "And somebody probably stole her."

"I know, I goofed," Bess cried. "And when I go to school without Autumn on Monday, the whole class will know!"

Nancy watched as Bess's eyes filled with tears.

"Ms. Franklin will be mad too," Bess went on.

"I'll never be able to shop for clothes at Darcy's again or visit Santa!"

Nancy wanted to find Autumn in time for school on Monday. But most of all she wanted to help her best friend!

"It's not Monday yet, Bess," Nancy said. "We have all weekend to find Autumn."

"Find her?" Bess sniffed.

"We're the Clue Crew, aren't we?" Nancy said with a smile. "So what are we waiting for? Let's look for clues!"

Nancy, Bess, and George got to work. They

first checked the porch for any hints to where Autumn might be. All Nancy saw was hay.

"It probably fell off Autumn," Nancy said, "when someone took her from the porch."

"That's not all that fell off," Bess said.

She picked up something from the top porch step. Nancy studied it in Bess's hand. It was red and round and the size of a small cookie.

"This wasn't here before," Bess said.

"How do you know?" George asked.

"Because I swept the porch before putting Autumn on it," Bess said. "I didn't want her clothes to get dirty."

Nancy took the red, round thing from Bess. It felt smooth and leathery. As Nancy flipped it over she saw two gold letters on the other side: an *H* and an *A*.

"'HA'?" Nancy read out loud.

"As if someone's laughing at us," George said. "I'll bet someone left it there on purpose."

"But who?" Bess cried.

Nancy had a pretty good idea. "I think the person who took Autumn was Deirdre," she said.

"It can't be Deirdre," Bess said. "Deirdre has tons of activities Saturday morning that she's always bragging about. She couldn't have been here while my mom and I were away."

"Oh," Nancy said.

They would have to think of more suspects. And the best place to do that was in their detective headquarters.

The Clue Crew headquarters was up in Nancy's room. Once they got there, George raced straight to her favorite tool—the computer on Nancy's desk.

"Okay," George said as she opened a case file. "Who do we think stole Autumn?"

"Besides Deirdre I'm not sure!" Nancy admitted.

"What about the boys?" Bess said. "They were mad because they couldn't make a sporty scarecrow."

"They also wanted a mascot for the soccer team," George added.

"Write that down, George," Nancy said. "Peter, Kevin, and Quincy are definitely suspects."

George entered the boys' names on their suspect list. "Done," she said. "Who else?"

Nancy tapped her chin as she thought and thought. But she couldn't get Deirdre off her mind.

"What kind of activities does Deirdre have on Saturday mornings?" Nancy asked.

Bess furrowed her brow. "I think she has ballet at nine, jewelry making at ten thirty—"

"Wait," Nancy interrupted. "About what time were you and your mom away from the house?"

"We left the house at nine," Bess said. "I know because my mom called out the car window, 'Bess—it's already nine o'clock, let's go!'"

"Deirdre would have been at ballet then," George said.

Suddenly Nancy had a hunch. "Find Deirdre's

ballet school on the computer, George," she said.

Nancy and Bess peered over George's shoulder as she pulled up the River Heights Ballet Academy's website. On the home page was a note that read: "CHILDREN'S BALLET CLASSES CANCELED FOR SATURDAY MORNING."

George read what was written underneath. "It says there are no classes because they're painting the studio."

"That's it!" Nancy said. "If Deirdre's ballet class was canceled, she could have gone to Bess's house after nine!"

"Do you really think Deirdre did it?" Bess asked.

"Deirdre was a sore loser when her design wasn't picked," Nancy explained. "And an even sorer loser when Autumn didn't wear Suki's clothes."

"She also said she would never shop at Darcy's again," Bess recalled. "Maybe stealing Autumn was a way to get even with the store."

"Let's see if Deirdre put Autumn's picture on

her dumb blog," George said.

Nancy watched as George pulled up Dishing with Deirdre. Sure enough, on the home page was the picture of Autumn.

Nancy stared at Autumn's picture on the computer. Underneath, Deirdre had written: "Soon this will all be mine!"

"Does that mean she planned to steal Autumn?" Bess gasped.

Nancy wasn't sure of that. But she was pretty sure of one thing. . . .

"Deirdre knows where we can find Autumn," Nancy said. "So let's find Deirdre."

It was eleven o'clock, so Deirdre would be at her jewelry-making class at Blings and Things.

Hannah had to run an errand, so she drove the girls to Main Street. While Hannah went into the supermarket, Nancy, Bess, and George waited outside Blings and Things for Deirdre.

"Pretty!" Bess said, gazing at the jewelry in the window. "After we nab her—can we go shopping?"

"Forget shopping," George said. "I want to grab a slice of pizza."

"Pizza this early?" Nancy asked.

"It's never too early for pizza," George said. She nodded at the restaurant across the street. "Pie in the Sky is already open for business."

Nancy glanced across the street. Above the pizza place was another store. A sign on the window read: DESIGNS BY SUKI.

"Suki," Nancy said slowly. "I wonder if it's the same Suki that Deirdre invited to school yesterday."

A woman suddenly appeared in the window—a woman with bright red hair and glasses!

"That's her all right," George said.

Suki carefully placed a hat on a stand in front of the window. That's when Nancy's eyes popped wide open.

"OMG, you guys." Nancy gasped. "That's Autumn's hat!"

CHAPTER FOUR

Sew Busted!

Suki stepped away from the window. The girls stood staring up at the hat.

"It's got to be the same hat," Bess said. "The flowers are exactly the same colors—dark red, orange, and gold."

"What does this have to do with Deirdre?" George asked.

"Maybe it wasn't Deirdre who stole the scarecrow," Nancy said. "Maybe the real culprit was Suki!"

"Why would Suki want to steal Autumn?" Bess asked.

"Maybe Deirdre asked her to," Nancy said.

"And Deirdre always gets what she wants, right?"

"Right!" Bess and George said together.

"Let's go in and see what's up," Nancy said.

The friends carefully crossed the street. They opened the door to Suki's studio and climbed the stairs. The door was half open, so the girls peeked inside. Suki's back was to the door as she reached for something on a shelf.

"I'll be right there with the pins!" Suki called.

Then, holding a small box, Suki slipped through a thick red curtain in the back of the room.

"Suki has a customer," Bess whispered. "If she's pinning up clothes, it should take a while."

"Good!" Nancy whispered. "That'll give us time to look for Autumn."

Nancy, Bess, and George quietly entered the studio. They spoke in whispers as they looked around.

"Wowee!" Bess said. "So this is what a fashion designer's studio looks like."

Nancy had never seen a fashion designer's studio either. There were two long tables. One had colorful fabric pinned to it. The smaller table had a sewing machine on top.

On the wall were sketches of clothes, probably designed by Suki. A dressmaker dummy stood on the side with no clothes on it, just a few pins stuck here and there.

"OMG!" Nancy gasped. She pointed to a pair of yellow boots next to the dummy. "Those are the boots Autumn wore!"

"There are the leggings!" George nodded at a pair of leggings draped over a chair. "But where's Autumn?"

Bess took the flowered hat off the stand. As she checked it out she said, "Something looks different."

"What?" Nancy asked.

"My little sister, Maggie, got a peanut butter stain on the inside of Autumn's hat," Bess said sheepishly. "This one has no stain."

Nancy was about to look at the hat when they heard Suki's voice say, "Why don't you try on the boots and hat?"

Nancy's stomach did a double flip. Suki was coming back! There was no time to run for the door—they had to hide.

"Under there!" George pointed to the sewing table.

The girls darted beneath the pale blue table skirt. It was long enough to cover them and short enough for them to see Suki's shoes go by—red-and-white polka-dotted flats.

"What's that for?" Bess whispered.

She pointed to a foot pedal on the floor. It was attached to a wire that ran under the skirt and up to the table.

"It's the pedal for the sewing machine," Nancy whispered. "Hannah has one just like it."

Another pair of feet appeared next to Suki's. They were smaller than Suki's and wore the yellow boots.

"I'm so glad my mother let me skip jewelry making for this!" a voice said.

Nancy, Bess, and George traded wide-eyed looks. The voice belonged to Deirdre. She wasn't in Blings and Things but in Suki's studio!

"Oh, and thanks for helping me, Suki," Deirdre added.

"No problem, Deirdre," Suki was saying. "That picture you took of Autumn really came in handy."

Nancy stared openmouthed at Bess and George. Did Deirdre take the picture so Suki would know what to steal?

"This will show Darcy's Department Store!" Deirdre said meanly. "This will show them good!"

Nancy narrowed her eyes. So that was it. Deirdre and Suki were partners in crime!

"That's funny," Suki said. "The hat was just here. Where did it go?"

Nancy stared at the hat in Bess's hand. There had been no time for her to put it back!

Suki's feet approached the table. Nancy wiggled farther back until—

WHHHHIIIIIIIRRRRRRR!

Nancy gave a little shriek as she realized what she had done—she had sat down on the foot pedal that made the sewing machine run!

"OMG!" Deirdre's voice cried over the noise. "The sewing machine—it's being used by a ghost!"

CHAPTER FIVE

Soccer Shocker

"Nancy, get off that thing!" George said as she yanked her off the foot pedal. It sent Nancy tumbling out from underneath the table.

"Nancy Drew!" Deirdre said. She narrowed her eyes. "And where there's Nancy—there's Bess and George!"

Deirdre lifted the table skirt and said, "Aha!"

Bess and George crawled out from underneath the table. Nancy knew they were busted, but so was Deirdre. Not only was she wearing Autumn's yellow boots; she was wearing her red coat, too.

"There's the hat I was looking for," Suki said, pointing to Bess's hands.

"What are you doing here?" Deirdre demanded.

Nancy glanced worriedly at Bess and George. If they said they were looking for Autumn, Deirdre would know the scarecrow was missing.

"Um, we came here to see Suki!" George blurted.

"Me?" Suki asked.

George nodded. "Bess watches *Catwalk Champs* all the time. She wants your autograph."

"I do?" Bess asked. When she got it, she quickly added, "Oh—I do! More than anything!"

"Thanks," Suki said, her brow furrowed. "But if you'll remember, I didn't win the contest."

"Who cares?" Nancy piped up. "Someday you'll be a famous fashion designer and that's what counts."

Deirdre stared at the girls with disbelief, but Suki's face was beaming.

"Well, of course you can have my autograph," Suki said graciously. "I'll be back with one for each of you."

"Great," George said.

Suki slipped away to find some paper. Deirdre glared at the girls and whispered, "If all you wanted was Suki's autograph, why were you hiding under the table?"

This time Nancy thought fast. . . .

"I was just showing Bess and George how a sewing machine works," Nancy said.

"Okay . . ." Deirdre said slowly. She pointed to the flowered hat in Bess's hands. "Then what are you doing with my hat?"

"You mean Autumn's," Bess said. She nodded at the clothes Deidre was wearing. "And her coat—and her boots!"

"They can't be from Darcy's," Nancy told Deirdre. "You said you'd never shop there again."

"And I meant it!" Deirdre said. "So I did something to get back at Darcy's in a huge way."

"What did you do?" Nancy asked slowly.

The girls waited for Deirdre to say that with the help of Suki she stole Autumn—and her clothes. Instead Deirdre grabbed the hat from Bess, put it on her head, and began to twirl.

"I asked Suki to make me the exact same outfit as Autumn's!" Deirdre declared.

Suki returned with a pen and paper. She had overheard what Deirdre had said and smiled.

"When fashion designers copy other designer's clothes, they're called knockoffs," Suki said.

"Knockoffs?" George repeated.

"That's why I took a picture of Autumn in her clothes," Deirdre said. "I wanted Suki to get the outfit just right."

"So that's what you meant on your blog?" Nancy asked. "That soon the *clothes* would be yours?"

"Of course the clothes!" Deirdre said, rolling her eyes. "You didn't think I wanted that silly scarecrow, did you?"

Nancy didn't know whether to believe Deirdre or not. While Suki signed her autographs, Nancy whispered to Bess and George, "How do we really know those clothes were made by Suki?"

"There *is* a way," Bess whispered.

Nancy and George followed Bess over to Deirdre.

"Hey!" Deirdre complained as Bess tugged at her collar. "What are you doing?"

Bess flipped over the collar to reveal a label. It read: "Designs by Suki."

"Autumn's clothes had the Darcy's Department Store label on them," Bess pointed out.

"Why do you care?" Deirdre demanded. "Did something happen to Autumn's clothes? Or . . . did something happen to Autumn?"

"No!" Nancy, Bess, and George said at the same time.

41

Deirdre's eyes suddenly flashed. "I have an idea. . . . Why don't I go over to Bess's house right now?" she said.

"Why?" Bess asked.

"So I can take another picture," Deirdre said. "A picture of me next to Autumn wearing the same clothes."

Nancy, Bess, and George stared openmouthed at Deirdre. If Deirdre went to Bess's house, she'd know there was no Autumn!

"Um . . . you can't take a picture," Nancy said.

"Why not?" Deirdre demanded.

"Autumn is very camera shy!" George blurted.

"But I already took a picture of her," Deirdre said. "Yesterday at school, remember?"

"Yeah, and she hated it," George said quickly.

"See you Monday!" Nancy said with a little wave.

"Wait!" Suki called as the girls charged out the door. "You forgot my autographs!"

As they raced down the stairs Bess said, "Did you see how Deirdre looked at us? She must know something is up!"

"We can't worry about Deirdre Shannon," Nancy said. "We have to keep looking for Autumn."

"Our next suspects are Kevin, Peter, and Quincy," George said as they walked outside.

"The boys," Bess said with a frown. "But where are we going to find *them*?"

"I'll bet their team, the Green Monsters, have a game today," George said. "Most of the soccer teams play in the park on Saturdays."

"Then the park is where we're going next!" Nancy said with a firm nod.

They had promised to meet Hannah in front of the supermarket. On the way they passed Darcy's Department Store. Ms. Franklin stood outside while workers hung colorful leaves in the window. She recognized Nancy, Bess, and George and smiled.

"We started dressing the window," Ms. Franklin

said excitedly. "All that's missing is your scare-crow."

"Missing?" Bess gasped. "How did you know—"

George jabbed Bess with her elbow. She then forced a smile and said, "Our scarecrow looks great, Ms. Franklin!"

"And so does your window so far," Nancy said.

Ms. Franklin smiled. "Every store window should be well dressed," she declared. "Especially in the fall!"

Nancy, Bess, and George said good-bye to Ms. Franklin before walking on.

"Good-bye, girls," Ms. Franklin called after them. "I can't wait to see your scarecrow on Monday!"

"Neither can we," George mumbled.

Hannah came out of the supermarket carry-ing bags of groceries. She was glad to drop the girls off at the park next.

Once there, the girls headed straight to the soccer field. Two other teams were playing but not the Green Monsters. The only boy they recognized was Tommy Maron from their class. Tommy stood alone dribbling a soccer ball.

"Hi, Tommy," Nancy said. "Do you know where Kevin, Peter, and Quincy went?"

"Why?" Tommy joked. "Do you *like* them?"

"Ewwwww!" Bess cried.

"Do you know or not, Maron?" George demanded.

"I think they went to Kevin's house," Tommy said. "They wanted to take home our new mascot."

Nancy, Bess, and George traded wide-eyed looks. Did Tommy just say *mascot*?

CHAPTER SIX

Hay, You!

"Is the mascot a scarecrow?" Nancy asked.

"Maybe," Tommy teased. "Maybe not."

Nancy rolled her eyes. Tommy was playing a game—and it wasn't soccer. "Come on, Tommy," she urged. "Tell us!"

"I've got to go," Tommy said, tucking the ball under his arm. "My dad is waiting for me."

"Phooey," Bess said as Tommy ran off. "Now we'll never know if their mascot was Autumn or not."

Nancy felt frustrated too. Until she remembered something about Kevin . . .

"Who says we won't?" Nancy said. "Kevin is

always bragging that he lives across the street from the park."

"So?" George said.

"So," Nancy said with a smile. "Next stop, the Garcias'!"

The girls left the park and carefully crossed the street. They read the names on the mailboxes until they found the Garcias'.

"If Kevin does have Autumn," Nancy said, "he's probably keeping her in his room."

"I'm not going in a boy's room!" Bess

complained. "You never know what gross things we'll find."

"As long as we find Autumn—who cares?" George said.

As they approached the house, they heard voices. They weren't coming from the house but from a tool shed next to it. The door was closed, making the voices hard to hear.

"Let's go closer," Nancy said quietly.

But then the door began to open. Quickly the girls hid behind a thick tree trunk.

Nancy, Bess, and George peeked out from behind the tree. As Kevin, Peter, and Quincy filed out they dusted what looked like yellow grass from their clothes.

"That looks like hay," Nancy whispered.

"Autumn is made of hay," Bess said. "Maybe she's in there!"

The girls watched Peter stuff bunches of hay up his sleeves. "I'm a scarecrow!" he began shouting. "Look at me, I'm a scarecrow!"

"Scarecrow, huh?" George whispered. "Something tells me we came to the right place."

The boys laughed as they tossed hay at one another. Kevin then said, "Let's shoot some hoops in my backyard."

The boys ran around the house. When the coast was clear, the girls stepped out from behind the tree.

"We've got to look inside," Nancy said.

"Yeah," George agreed. "I have a feeling we'll find a lot more than tools."

Luckily Kevin had left the shed door open, so the girls slipped inside.

"Where are you, Autumn?" Bess called. "Come out, come out, wherever you are."

They found gardening tools, a lawn mower, bags of planting soil, and more hay scattered on the floor. But where was Autumn?

"Look!" Bess suddenly cried.

She pointed to a row of metal shelves against one wall. On one of the shelves was a long cardboard box. Written on the side were the words: "Most Awesome Mascot in the World!"

"That box is big enough to fit Autumn," George said. "I'm looking inside."

Nancy, Bess, and George moved toward the shelf. Suddenly the box began to wiggle. The sounds of scratching and bumping came from inside too!

"You guys." Bess gulped. "If Autumn is in there . . . she's alive."

George led the way as the girls inched toward the shelf. Reaching up, George pulled at the box only to have it tip on its side. Bess shrieked. Clumps of hay began to drop out of the box all over the girls!

"Ewwww!" Nancy cried.

But that wasn't all. After a shower of hay came something big, fat, furry—and definitely alive.

"It's a giant rat!" Bess shrieked.

The creature dropped off Bess's shoulder onto Nancy's foot. She was about to scream too when she realized it wasn't a rat at all. In fact, it looked just like one of their class pets.

"It's a guinea pig, you guys!" Nancy said with a smile. She gently picked it up when the boys charged into the shed.

"What are you doing with our mascot?" Peter demanded.

The startled guinea pig leaped out of Nancy's hands, landing on the floor. He kicked up his feet before ricocheting around the shed.

"Get him!" Kevin cried.

The kids scrambled around the shed trying to catch the guinea pig. Heads bumped. Tools crashed to the floor. But the guinea pig was too fast to grab!

"We thought you wanted a scarecrow as a

mascot," Nancy shouted as the chase went on.

"We did!" Quincy shouted back. "But not a girlie-girl one like that Autumn."

"So my mom bought me Vinnie," Kevin said. "Guinea pigs make awesome mascots when they're not making a mess."

"Gotcha!" George said as she grabbed the guinea pig. She handed him to Kevin, who put him right back into his box.

"If Vinnie's so awesome," Bess said, "why is he living in a stinky cardboard box?"

"He won't be there for long," Peter said.

"My dad is building an awesome guinea pig habitat," Kevin explained. "It's going to have tunnels and caves—even a slide."

"He deserves it," Quincy said. "We already won a game today thanks to Vinnie."

Nancy believed the boys about their new mascot. But could they have still stolen Autumn?

"What time was your game?" Nancy asked.

The boys seemed surprised at the question.

"Nine thirty," Quincy answered. "But we

were in the park warming up at nine."

"Why do you want to know?" Kevin said, raising an eyebrow. "And why were you snooping in my dad's shed?"

"Are you spies for the *girls* soccer team?" Quincy demanded.

Nancy shot Bess and George a sideways glance. If they told the boys they were looking for Autumn, they'd know she was missing.

"We were looking for hay!" George said quickly.

"Autumn is way too skinny," Bess said. "She needs fattening up."

Nancy scooped up a handful of hay and said, "This is all we need, thanks."

Nancy, Bess, and George left the shed in a hurry.

"If the boys were at the park at nine, they couldn't have been at Bess's house stealing Autumn," Nancy said.

"We didn't find Autumn in there anyway," George said.

"That's the problem!" Bess wailed, raising her arms. "We're not finding Autumn anywhere!"

Nancy dusted the hay off her hands. She looked at her watch and said, "No wonder we can't find Autumn."

"Why?" George asked.

"Because it's way past lunchtime," Nancy said with a smile. "Who can solve mysteries on empty stomachs?"

"You're right," Bess said, smiling too. "Let's go to my house for tuna sandwiches with pickle relish."

"Pickle relish?" George said. She rubbed her hands together hungrily. "Bring it!"

As the girls neared the Marvin house, they noticed someone sitting on the porch steps. But it wasn't Autumn who'd returned. It was Deirdre Shannon!

"What's she doing here?" Bess whispered.

Sitting alongside Deirdre were two girls from the other third-grade class, Ashley McCoy and Valerie Noh.

"What's up?" Nancy asked.

"I told Ashley and Valerie about our class scarecrow," Deirdre said. "I thought you could show her to them."

Deirdre flashed a sly smile and said, "Unless . . . Autumn isn't here."

CHAPTER SEVEN

Farm Alarm

Deirdre, Ashley, and Valerie stood waiting for an answer. Finally George shrugged and said, "Yeah . . . Autumn is here."

"Huh?" Nancy and Bess said at the same time. Why was George saying something that wasn't true?

"Then let's see her," Deirdre said.

"Sure," George said. "We just have to get the mice out first."

"Mice?" Deirdre said.

"Mice love hay just like guinea pigs do," George explained. "We heard something squeak inside Autumn this morning."

Nancy tried hard not to giggle. She knew

George was making the mouse up. So did Bess. But Deirdre, Ashley, and Valerie did not!

"Ewww!" Ashley cried.

"If that scarecrow has a mouse living inside, I sure don't want to see it," Valerie declared.

"Geez, Deirdre," Ashley said as she and Valerie began walking away. "What were you thinking?"

As Deirdre followed her friends she looked back and scowled.

"She definitely suspects something," Bess whispered. "Next she'll be writing stuff about us on her silly blog."

"Who reads her dopey blog anyway?" George scoffed. "Now, where are those tuna sandwiches with pickle relish?"

They were about to head inside when a rustling noise filled the air.

"What was that?" Nancy asked.

"I think it came from over there," Bess said. She pointed to the hedge between the yard and the sidewalk.

"Give me a break," Nancy whispered. "Deidre is probably crouched down behind there listening in on us."

"Hey, I've got an idea." George snickered. "Let's sneak up on that spy and give her a scare."

The girls crouched too as they inched their way to the hedge. They were about to pop up and yell "Boo" when something popped up first—a big straw hat!

"Jake McStuffings!" Bess screamed.

The girls stared at the hat above the hedge until it dropped back down.

"Come on," George said. "If it is Jake—I want to see him with my own eyes!"

Bess unwillingly followed George and Nancy as they raced out of the yard onto the sidewalk. They peeked behind the hedge and saw no one. But then Bess pointed down the sidewalk and shouted, "Over there!"

Nancy turned and saw a shadowy figure racing to the end of the sidewalk. He was dressed in baggy clothes and a big straw hat.

There goes Jake,   George said.

"It wasn't Jake," Nancy said, shaking her head.

"Then who was it, Nancy?" Bess asked.

"I don't know," Nancy admitted. "I just know there is no such thing as a walking scarecrow."

But as the girls walked slowly to the Marvins' yard, Nancy glanced back at the hedge.

. . . *At least I hope there isn't,* Nancy thought.

"Daddy, do you believe in scary stories?" Nancy asked as she set the table for dinner later that day. "You know, like witches . . . werewolves . . . walking scarecrows?"

"Sure, I believe in scary stories, Nancy," Mr. Drew said, throwing her a wink. "But only on Halloween!"

Nancy did the math. Halloween was over three weeks away. Not only was it getting dark early—it was getting spooky.

"And speaking of Halloween," Mr. Drew said. "How about a trip to Granny Apple Farms tomorrow morning? You can ask Bess and George to come along too."

"Thanks, Daddy, but we can't," Nancy said. "The Clue Crew is working on a special case."

Hannah smiled as she carried a bowl of veggies into the dining room. "When isn't the Clue Crew working on something special?" she teased.

"This case is different, Hannah," Nancy said. "We have to solve it by Monday . . . or else."

"Hmm," Mr. Drew said. "I guess that is more important than a hayride."

"Hayride?" Nancy asked. She loved hayrides!

"And picking out the perfect pumpkin," Mr. Drew added.

"Pumpkin?" Nancy asked. She loved pumpkin picking!

Nancy thought about the farm as she folded another napkin in half.

"I guess the Clue Crew could use a break, Daddy," Nancy decided. "And maybe some yummy caramel apples too!"

Sunday morning Mr. Drew drove Nancy, Bess, and George to Granny Apple Farms. The three friends sat in the backseat whispering about what they saw the day before. . . .

"I didn't sleep all night," Bess said. "I kept thinking of that thing we saw outside my house."

"You mean Jake McStuffings?" George said.

Nancy heaved a sigh. "There is only one scarecrow we're going to talk about today," she said. "And her name is Autumn."

Mr. Drew pulled into the parking lot.

"Why don't you girls go ahead to the pumpkin patch while I pick up some apple cider?" he said as they climbed out of the car.

"Sure, Daddy," Nancy said.

Nancy, Bess, and George headed across the farm toward the pumpkin patch. On the way they passed stands selling apples, fresh veggies, and cider that smelled like cinnamon. Nancy was about to check out some colorful Indian corn when she heard the clip-clopping sound of horses' hooves.

Turning, Nancy smiled. It was a hay wagon being pulled by a horse. A bunch of smiling kids sat swinging their feet over the sides. Two girls wore identical pumpkin-colored jackets. Nancy recognized one of them from school.

"There's Leanne!" Nancy pointed out.

"She's with her little sister, Trixie," Bess said. "I guess Leanne likes hayrides too."

"How can she?" Nancy said. "She told Mrs. Ramirez she's allergic to hay."

"Maybe the wagon is filled with straw," Bess

said. "Leanne never said she was allergic to straw."

"You're probably right," Nancy said. "Now let's check out the pumpkins before the perfect ones are taken."

The friends hurried to the patch. It was filled with pumpkins and kids trying to lift them.

"How about that one?" George asked, pointing one out.

"Too big," Nancy said.

"How about that one?" Bess asked, pointing to another.

"Too small," Nancy said.

"Okay, Goldilocks," George joked. "Which one is just right?"

"How about that one?" a voice said.

The girls spun around. Standing right behind them was Harvey Mueller.

"Hi, Harvey," Nancy said. She hoped he wouldn't bring up Jake McStuffings!

"That pumpkin over there is perfect," Harvey said, pointing to a medium-sized pumpkin. "It's the right size and not as warped as some of the others."

"Thanks," George said.

Harvey then turned to Bess. "You should get a whole bunch of pumpkins," he said.

"Me?" Bess asked. "Why?"

"Because," Harvey said with a grin. "They would look awesome on your porch."

Bess stared at Harvey as he walked away. "How did Harvey know I have a porch?" she asked. "He never came to my house."

Nancy watched Harvey leave the pumpkin patch. He was pretty mad when no one believed his latest story. How far would he go to make everybody believe in Jake McStuffings?

"Maybe Harvey did come to your house, Bess," Nancy said. "Maybe he came to steal Autumn."

ChAPTER EiGhT

Bats and Hats

"Why would Harvey steal our scarecrow?" George asked.

"Maybe Harvey stole Autumn so we would think Jake did it," Nancy figured.

"Yeah," Bess said thoughtfully. "How else would Harvey know I had a porch unless he was there?"

"That's why I think Harvey Mueller is our next suspect," Nancy declared.

The girls looked all over the farm for Harvey but couldn't find him anywhere.

"He probably went home." Bess sighed.

"Then we should go to Harvey's house too,"

Nancy declared. "After we pick out a pumpkin and go on our hayride."

"I know where Harvey lives," George said. "We went to his Halloween party when we were in first grade, remember?"

"How can I forget?" Bess groaned. "Instead of apples we bobbed for rubber eyeballs."

Nancy remembered too. Harvey's house was four blocks away from hers and within walking distance.

After another hour of pumpkins, hayrides, and caramel apples it was time to get back to work. . . .

"Have fun at your friend Harvey's house!" Mr. Drew called from the car window.

George wrinkled her nose at the word "friend."

"Thanks, Daddy," Nancy called back.

The Clue Crew walked up toward the Mueller house. Nancy looked down and saw strands of hay scattered on the grass.

"That probably fell off Autumn when Harvey carried her here," Nancy said.

The girls followed the trail around the Muellers' house. It stopped suddenly at the base of a tree.

"Huh?" Nancy wondered.

But when the girls looked way up, they gasped. Up in the tree was a tree house—a haunted-looking tree house!

"Cheese and crackers!" George exclaimed.

The tree house had a crooked wooden roof and windows covered with cobwebs. A ladder leading up to the door was made of fake bones—at least Nancy hoped they were fake!

"If the trail of hay stops here," Nancy thought out loud, "then Harvey must have carried Autumn up to his tree house."

George cupped both hands around her mouth. "Come on out, Harvey Mueller," she shouted up to the tree house. "We want to talk to you!"

No answer.

"Harvey?" Nancy called up too.

Still no answer.

"Let's go up and look for Autumn," Nancy decided.

"But I'm afraid!" Bess wailed.

"Of heights?" Nancy asked.

"No!" Bess cried. "Of ghosts!"

"Get a grip, Bess," George said as she grabbed the ladder. "Whoever heard of a haunted tree house anyway?"

The bony ladder creaked as George climbed up first, followed by Nancy and then by Bess. Soon all three friends were inside and looking around.

"Whoa," George said.

Rubber bats and cobwebs hung from the ceiling. A green chair shaped like a monster claw stood next to a pile of scary books and movies. On a shelf were jars filled with rubber insects and plastic fangs.

"There's some more hay," Nancy said, pointing to the floor. "But where's Autumn?"

Bess gasped as a rubber bat swung against her head. They were about to look around some more when they heard a loud—

CREEEEAKKKK!

The girls froze. It was the ladder outside creaking.

"Someone's coming up," Nancy said.

"It's probably Harvey," Bess said.

Nancy, Bess, and George walked to the door and looked down. Someone was climbing up the ladder. All they could see was a big straw hat. The same hat they spotted behind the hedge yesterday!

Nancy felt her knees begin to shake.

She hadn't really believed in Harvey's walking scarecrow story—until now!

"Oh nooooo!" Nancy cried. "It's Jake McStuffings—and he's coming after us!"

CHAPTER NINE

Harvey's Secret

The girls backed away from the door. They grabbed anything they could find to throw at Jake—a monster mask, an alien action figure. George tried to pick up the monster claw chair, but it was too heavy. Instead she lifted the plastic jar of fangs.

"On your mark, get set—hurl!" George shouted.

Outside the door the hat came into view. Followed by the figure of—

"Harvey?" Bess said.

"Hey," Harvey said, stepping into the tree house. Along with the hat he wore baggy overalls and a checkered shirt—its sleeves stuffed with hay!

Nancy couldn't believe her eyes. Harvey Mueller was dressed as a scarecrow!

"What are you doing up here?" George asked.

"It's my tree house!" Harvey exclaimed. "What are you doing up here?"

The girls dropped what they were holding.

"First tell us why you look just like Jake McStuffings!" Nancy demanded.

"Uh . . . I am Jake McStuffings," Harvey blurted.

"Say what?" George asked.

"Every fall I jump off my pole," Harvey said

in a hushed voice. "To roam the streets of—"

"Liar, liar, pants on fire!" Bess said, jumping up and down. "You are not Jake McStuffings and you know it."

"You're just pretending to be Jake," Nancy demanded. "Aren't you, Harvey?"

"I guess you could say that," Harvey said.

"So that was you dancing around in Nancy's yard on Friday?" George demanded. "And hiding behind Bess's hedge yesterday?"

"I guess you could say that, too," Harvey said sheepishly.

"No wonder you knew I had a porch," Bess muttered.

Nancy frowned at Harvey. She planted both hands on her hips and said, "Why would you want to scare us like that?"

Harvey waved his hay-stuffed arms in the air.

"I wanted everyone to think Jake was real," Harvey explained. "I was sick of getting laughed at for my scary stories."

"You know what's really scary, Harvey

Mueller?" Bess said angrily. "Not knowing what happened to Autumn!"

Harvey wrinkled his nose. "What do you mean?"

"Don't act dumb, Harvey," George said. "You were sneaking around everyone's yards all weekend. You probably sneaked away with Autumn!"

"Are you saying I stole her?" Harvey gasped.

"Well?" Bess said. "Did you?"

Harvey shook his head. "All I wanted to do was pretend to be Jake," he insisted. "Cross my heart and hope to croak, drop an eyeball in my Coke!"

"Ew!" Bess said.

Nancy studied Harvey and almost believed him. She just had one more question. . . .

"Where were you at nine o'clock on Saturday morning?" Nancy asked.

"That's easy," Harvey said. "I was on Main Street with my mom buying new sneakers."

Nancy glanced down at Harvey's clean, white

sneakers. Even the laces looked new.

"If you don't believe me," Harvey went on, "ask Mr. Allen at the Shoe Shack. He'll tell you that I was there."

Harvey then grabbed a jar and said, "While you're here, do you want to try on some fangs? I washed the spit off just yesterday."

"No, thank you!" Bess blurted.

"And before we leave," Nancy said, "promise us you'll never pretend to be Jake McStuffings again."

"No fair!" Harvey exclaimed. "What am I going to do with all these scarecrow clothes?"

"Halloween's coming," George called as the girls climbed down the ladder. "I'm sure you'll need a costume!"

The girls walked away from the Mueller house. Nancy was certain Harvey told the truth about Autumn, but Bess still wasn't sure.

"Let's talk to Mr. Allen at the Shoe Shack," Bess said. "If Harvey made up Jake McStuffings, he could have made up buying new sneakers too."

"But his sneakers did look new," Nancy said.

"Pleeeeeease?" Bess said. "Tomorrow is Monday. There isn't much time left to find Autumn!"

"Okay," Nancy agreed. She didn't think they would find anything new. But Bess was getting frantic.

Nancy, Bess, and George walked from Harvey's house to Main Street. On the way to the Shoe Shack they stopped at Darcy's to check out the fall window. The colorful leaves were hung in place. A few pumpkins were scattered over a floor covered with hay.

"I wonder where they'll put Autumn," George said.

"If we ever find Autumn!" Bess said sadly.

"The day isn't over yet, Bess," Nancy said gently. "We still have time to find our scarecrow."

As they turned away from the window Nancy glanced across the street at Hudson's Apparel. They didn't have a fancy store window like Darcy's—only suitcases and a stuffed squirrel like Leanne said.

Just then a woman and a small girl stepped  out of the revolving doors. Nancy recognized the girl and her pumpkin-colored jacket.

"There's Leanne's sister, Trixie," Nancy pointed out.

But as Nancy looked harder she recognized something

else—the big flowered hat on the little girl's head!

"You guys," Nancy said. "Isn't that the hat Autumn wore?"

"Trixie probably got one at Darcy's Department Store," George said. "Autumn didn't have the only one."

"But Trixie's parents own Hudson's Apparel," Nancy said. "If Leanne doesn't shop at Darcy's, why would Trixie?"

Then Nancy remembered something else. . . .

"Leanne was on a hayride when she's supposed to be allergic to hay," Nancy said slowly.

"So?" George asked.

"So maybe Leanne didn't want to help make our scarecrow for a reason," Nancy said. Her eyes flashed as she stared at her friends. "Maybe *she* had something to do with Autumn disappearing!"

"What do we do, Nancy?" Bess asked.

Nancy looked across the street. Trixie and her mom were turning the corner.

"We follow Trixie," Nancy said urgently, "and get a better look at that hat!"

ChAPTER TEN

Tea for a Clue

Nancy, Bess, and George tried not to let Mrs. Hudson or Trixie know they were being followed. They walked several feet behind them, ducking behind trees every time Trixie looked back.

Finally Trixie and her mom turned into the front lawn of a white house with a red roof and shutters.

"There's Leanne," Nancy said.

She could see Leanne jumping rope in her front yard. She kept playing as her mom and sister entered the house.

"Hi, Leanne!" Bess called.

Leanne stopped as the girls walked over. She blinked with surprise before saying, "Hi."

"We saw you on a hayride today," Nancy said. "I guess your hay allergy must be better."

"Um . . . k-k-kind of," Leanne stammered.

Nancy could tell Leanne was nervous—as if she had something to hide.

"If your allergy is better," Nancy said. "Then you'll have no trouble being around scarecrows."

Leanne dropped her jump rope on the grass. "I don't know where Autumn is!" she said. "I didn't steal her—if that's what you're thinking."

Nancy stared at Leanne. "I never said Autumn was missing," she said. "Or stolen."

"So how did you know?" George asked.

"I can't talk anymore," Leanne said quickly. "I promised Trixie I'd help out with her tea party."

"Is that why Trixie is wearing such a fancy hat?" Bess asked. "The same hat as Autumn's?"

"I told you, I've got to go!" Leanne insisted. She picked up her jump rope and ran straight into the house.

Nancy, Bess, and George stood staring at the house.

"How are we going to get to Leanne's room to see if Autumn is there?" George asked.

"Good question." Nancy sighed.

"Wait," Bess said. "Do you hear someone?"

The girls became quiet.

That's when Nancy heard someone singing "I'm a Little Teapot."

"It's coming from behind the house!" Nancy said.

"Everything lately is behind the house," George groaned. She waved toward the back. "Come on, let's check it out."

Nancy, Bess, and George rounded the corner to see a garden filled with fall chrysanthemums. In the middle of the garden was a table covered with a lacy tablecloth, a vase of yellow flowers, and a toy tea set.

"It's Trixie's tea party," Bess whispered.

Trixie sat in one of the chairs, her back to the girls. She kept singing as she poured for her guests: a doll, a stuffed giraffe, a teddy bear, and—a scarecrow!

"It's Autumn!" Nancy gasped.

The Clue Crew marched straight to the table. When Trixie saw them she scowled. "You again?" she snapped. "Get away from my toys!"

"We don't want your toys!" George said. "Just our scarecrow."

Trixie jumped up as George lifted Autumn out of her chair. "Let go!" Trixie shouted. "Leanne gave me the scarecrow fair and square. It's mine!"

"It's ours!" George said, holding Autumn.

Trixie grabbed Autumn's legs and began to pull. George pulled back. Soon Nancy and Bess were watching a full-blown scarecrow tug-of-war!

"Stop!" Bess cried as straw flew everywhere. "You're going to break her!"

A back door swung open. Leanne raced outside with a plate of cookies. She took one look at the tug-of-war and shouted, "Quit it, you guys. Quit it right now!"

George and Trixie dropped Autumn. Instead of picking the scarecrow up, Trixie ran crying into the house.

Leanne stared down at Autumn. "Um . . . what's a scarecrow doing in my yard?" She gulped.

"Why don't you tell us?" Bess said.

"Maybe it walked over here!" Leanne said quickly. "Just like that scarecrow Harvey was talking about."

"Harvey admitted that Jake wasn't for real," George said.

"Oh," Leanne said, casting her eyes downward.

"Why did you do it, Leanne?" Nancy asked gently. "Why did you take Autumn?"

"I was afraid everyone would shop at Darcy's Department Store because of that silly window," Leanne said. "And no one would come to my family's store anymore."

"So you took the best part of the window— the scarecrow," Nancy said.

"How did you know it was on my porch?" Bess asked.

"I was wheeling home a new suitcase from Hudson's Apparel," Leanne explained. "We have tons of suitcases at home."

"Go on!" George urged.

"I saw a scarecrow on a porch," Leanne said. "I didn't know it was Bess's porch, but I knew it was our scarecrow from the clothes it was wearing."

"That's when you took her?" Bess asked.

Leanne nodded as she placed the plate of cookies on the table.

"I put Autumn inside the suitcase and wheeled her home," Leanne explained. "You'd be surprised what fits inside a Hudson's Apparel suitcase."

Hudson's Apparel, Nancy thought. *H . . . A!*

Nancy pulled the red, round *HA* out of her jacket pocket. "Did this come from Hudson's too?" she asked.

"Yes!" Leanne said. "Those tags are on all of our suitcases. It must have fallen off when I was trying to put Autumn inside."

"No wonder they're on sale," George muttered.

"I'm really sorry," Leanne cried. "You guys are great detectives . . . but I'm a terrible classmate."

Tears welled in Leanne's eyes as she said, "I even lied about being allergic to hay so I wouldn't have to make a scarecrow for Darcy's."

"You're not terrible, Leanne," Nancy said with a smile. "You made a mistake and everybody makes mistakes."

"Even me," Bess said. "I left the scarecrow on the porch when I should have kept her inside. So we're even!"

Leanne finally smiled. "I was going to bring

Autumn back after Trixie's tea party," she said. "Honest!"

"What's important is that we found Autumn," Nancy said. "And just in time for school tomorrow."

"Yippee!" Bess cheered. "This calls for another celebration!"

"Totally!" Leanne agreed. She smiled at the pretty table in the garden and said, "Tea party, anyone?"

Monday morning Bess brought Autumn to school as promised. Later that week the whole class gathered on Main Street for the unveiling of Darcy's new fall window.

"She's perfect!" Bess swooned when they saw Autumn seated on a bale of hay surrounded by pumpkins.

"I hope you got the mouse out," Deirdre muttered.

Nancy, Bess, and George ignored Deirdre. The important thing was that Autumn was where she belonged—in the window of Darcy's Department Store!

"Well done, boys and girls!" Ms. Franklin announced. "Now everyone will want to shop at Darcy's Department Store."

"That's what I was afraid of," Leanne whispered.

Nancy felt bad for Leanne. She looked across the street at Hudson's Apparel and their boring store window. That's when she got an idea. . . .

"Leanne—why don't we design a window just for Hudson's?" Nancy asked. "Something other than luggage and a stuffed squirrel?"

"Yes!" Bess said excitedly. "We can dress up some mannequins in Hudson's prettiest fall clothes—"

"And put them on a hayride!" George suggested.

Leanne's eyes shone brightly. "My mom and dad will love the idea!" she said. "But why do you want to do it?"

Nancy remembered what Mimi Franklin said and smiled.

"Because *every* store window should be well dressed," Nancy declared. "Especially in the fall!"

PAPER PLATE SCARECROW

What's the dish on making a great scarecrow?
You don't need hay or straw. Just a paper plate,
a few fun crafts—and lots of imagination!

Materials

- 1 Paper plate
- 2 Plastic eyes or round buttons
- Bunches of hair-colored yarn
- Colorful markers or crayons
- Orange, red, or brown construction paper
- Glue

- Red or orange ribbon
- Scissors

Directions

Glue yarn at the top of the plate to make the hair.

Cut construction paper in the shape of a hat. Glue the hat on the top of the plate.

To make a face, glue plastic eyes or buttons onto the plate.

Draw on a triangle-shaped nose.

Underneath the nose draw a cheery smile.

Tie the ribbon into a bow and glue it on the bottom of the plate.

Add your own special touches like rosy-red cheeks or a sprinkle of freckles. Or glam up the hat with feathers, stickers—even autumn leaves!

When your scarecrow is done, hang it on the front door. It's the perfect welcome for friends—*and for fall!*

NaNcy DReW aND The cLUe cReW®

Test your detective skills with more Clue Crew cases!

FROM ALaDDiN • PUbLiSHeD By SiMoN & ScHUSTeR